E                                    99-66
T    Thomas, Shelley Moore
     Somewhere today

E                                    99-66
T    Thomas, Shelley Moore
     Somewhere today

# Somewhere Today

## A Book of Peace

### SHELLEY MOORE THOMAS

*photographs by* ERIC FUTRAN

ALBERT WHITMAN & COMPANY

MORTON GROVE, ILLINOIS

99-66

Thanks to all the children and adults who appear in this book. Special thanks to Susan Futran, who arranged and coordinated the shooting.

Library of Congress Cataloging-in-Publication Data

Thomas, Shelley Moore.
Somewhere today: a book of peace / by Shelley Moore Thomas;
photographs by Eric Futran.
p. cm.

*Summary:* Gives examples of ways in which people bring about peace
by doing things to help and care for one another and their world.

ISBN 0-8075-7545-3
1. Helping behavior—Juvenile literature. [1. Helpfulness. 2. Caring.]
I. Futran, Eric, ill. II. Title.
BF637.H4T48 1998
811'.54—dc21 97-27867
CIP
AC

Text copyright © 1998 by Shelley Moore Thomas.
Photographs copyright © 1998 by Eric Futran.
Published in 1998 by Albert Whitman & Company,
6340 Oakton Street, Morton Grove, Illinois 60053-2723.
Published simultaneously in Canada by General Publishing, Limited, Toronto.

Printed in the United States of America.
10 9 8 7 6 5 4 3 2 1

The design is by Scott Piehl.

For Isabelle, Noel, Ellie, John, Hope,
Mia, and Jacob. Take care of each other.
—S. M. T.

To Susan, who makes all good
things possible.
—E. F.

# Somewhere today...

someone

is

being

a

friend

instead

of

fighting.

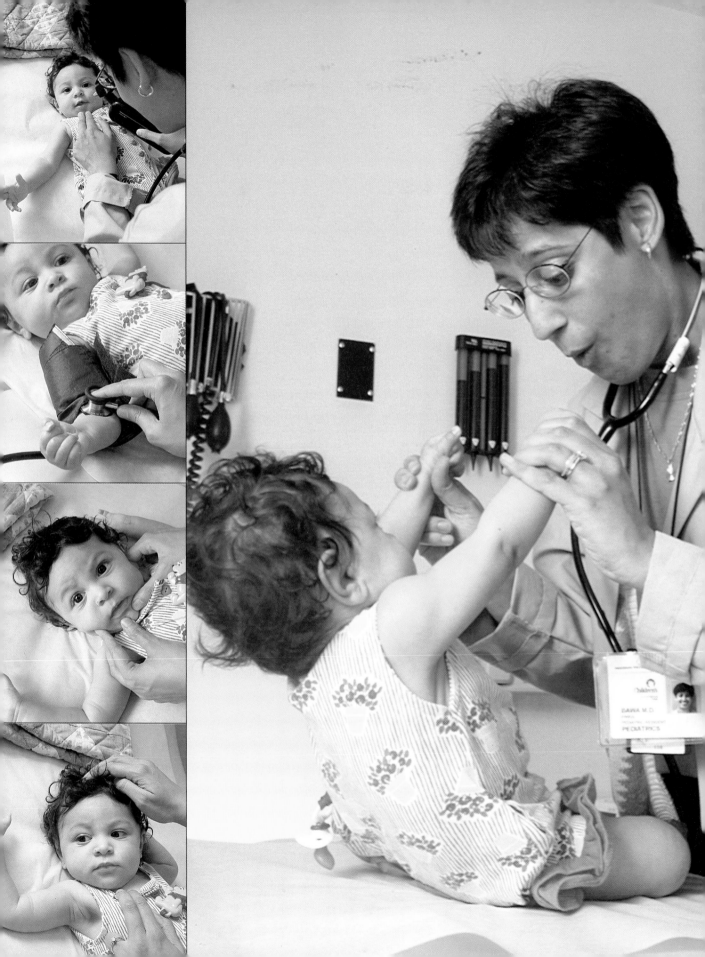

# Somewhere today...

someone

is

caring

for

a

child

so

she

won't

get

sick.

someone

is

joining

a

friend's

celebration.

# Somewhere today...

# Somewhere today...

someone

is

teaching

his

little

sister

to

ride

a

bike.

# Somewhere today...

someone

is

getting

a

letter

from

far

away.

someone

is

visiting

a

friend

who

is

old.

Somewhere today...

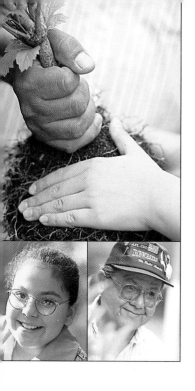

someone

is

planting

a

tree

where

one

Somewhere was today...

cut

down.

someone

is

fixing

old

toys

Somewhere today...

to

give

to

new

friends.

someone

is

learning

Somewhere today...
to

do

things

a

different

way.

someone

is

reading

a

Somewhere today...

book

about

peace

and

thinking

about

making

the

world

a

better

place.

Maybe it is you.